THIS WALKER BOOK BELONGS TO:

_____

_____

_____

For Rosie
who lent me her babies,
Lucy and Nicola
M.W.

For Ruth
and Rowan,
my real inspiration
P.D.

First published 1990 by Walker Books Ltd, 87 Vauxhall Walk, London SE11 5HJ

Text © 1990 Martin Waddell   Illustrations © 1990 Penny Dale

The right of Martin Waddell and Penny Dale to be identified as
author and illustrator respectively of this work has been asserted by them
in accordance with the Copyright, Designs and Patents Act 1988

This edition published 1992

16 18 20 19 17

Printed in China   All rights reserved

British Library Cataloguing in Publication Data:
a catalogue record for this book is available from the British Library

ISBN-13: 978-0-7445-2335-5
ISBN-10: 0-7445-2335-4

www.walkerbooks.co.uk

Rosie's Babies

Written by
Martin Waddell

Illustrated by
Penny Dale

WALKER BOOKS
AND SUBSIDIARIES
LONDON · BOSTON · SYDNEY · AUCKLAND

Mum was putting the baby
to bed and Rosie said,
"I've got two babies and
you've only got one."
"Two, including you," said Mum.
"I'm not a baby, I'm four years old,"
said Rosie.
"Tell me about your babies,"
Mum said.

And Rosie said,
"My babies live in a bird's nest
and they are nearly as big as me.
They go out in the garden all by
themselves and sometimes they
make me cross!"
"Do they?" said Mum.
"Yes, when they do silly things!"
said Rosie.
"What silly things do they do?"
asked Mum.

And Rosie said,
"My babies climbed a big
mountain. That was silly, because
they couldn't get down. They
jumped, and they bumped on
their bottoms!"
"Silly babies," said Mum.
"Did they hurt themselves?"

And Rosie said,
"One of my babies hurt her knee.
I bandaged it up and she cried
and I said 'Never mind'
because I am kind."
"I'm sure you are," said Mum.
"What else do your babies do?"

And Rosie said,
"My babies drive cars that
are real ones and lorries and
dumpers and boats. My babies
are very good drivers."
"What do your babies like
doing best?" asked Mum.

And Rosie said,
"My babies like swings and
rockers and dinosaurs. They go
to the park when it's dark and
there are no mums and dads
who can see, only me!"
"Gracious!" said Mum.
"Aren't they scared?"

And Rosie said,
"My babies are scared of the
big dog, but I'm not.
I know the big dog. I go
'Blackie, sit,' and he does."
"They are not very scared then?"
said Mum.
"My babies know I will look
after them," said Rosie.
"I'm their mum."
"How do you look after them?"
Mum asked.

And Rosie said,
"I make their teas and I tell them stories and I take them for walks and I talk to them and I tell them that I love them."

"That's a good way to look after babies!" said Mum. "Do you make them nice things to eat, like pies?"

And Rosie said,
"My babies make their own pies,
 but they never eat them."
"What do they eat?" asked Mum.

And Rosie said,
"My babies eat apples and apples
and apples all the time. And
grapes and pears but they
don't like the pips."
"Most babies don't," said Mum.
"Are you going to tell me
more about your babies?"

And Rosie thought and thought and thought and then Rosie said, "My babies have gone to bed." "Just like this one," said Mum. "I don't want to talk about my babies any more because they are asleep," said Rosie. "I don't want them to wake up, or they'll cry." "We could talk very softly," said Mum.

"Yes," said Rosie.

"What will we talk about?" asked Mum.

And Rosie said,
"ME!"

WALKER BOOKS is the world's leading independent publisher of children's books. Working with the best authors and illustrators we create books for all ages, from babies to teenagers – books your child will grow up with and always remember. So…

FOR THE BEST CHILDREN'S BOOKS, LOOK FOR THE BEAR